SHELL HUNTER

By Carl Geren

Illustrations by John Maggard

 CHILDRENS PRESS, CHICAGO

Library of Congress Cataloging in Publication Data

Geren, Carl.
    Shell hunter.
    SUMMARY: While hunting for food, a young boy
demonstrates the value of his shell whistles.
    [1. Man, Prehistoric—Fiction] I. Maggard, John.
II. Title.
PZ7.G2945Sh   [E]   76-39962
ISBN 0-516-03611-4

For almost an hour Targ had sat quietly
before the little cave fire. His hands moved
with skill as orange flames made shadows on
the cave walls. The cold winds told of the
coming ice-age winter.

Targ turned his wrist one more time. The tip of his flint knife made a second hole in the tiny shell. He put the knife back under his leather belt. Then he raised the shell to his lips and blew on its open end. It made only a small whistling sound. But it was pleasant and musical. The sound was like the sound of the rippling brook waters from which the shell had come.

Targ held the shell forward and let the fire glow on its colorful surface. He smiled. It was too bad that such beautiful trinkets had no real value. Targ wore them only as ornaments on a grass string about his neck. Each had its own special color and its own sound.

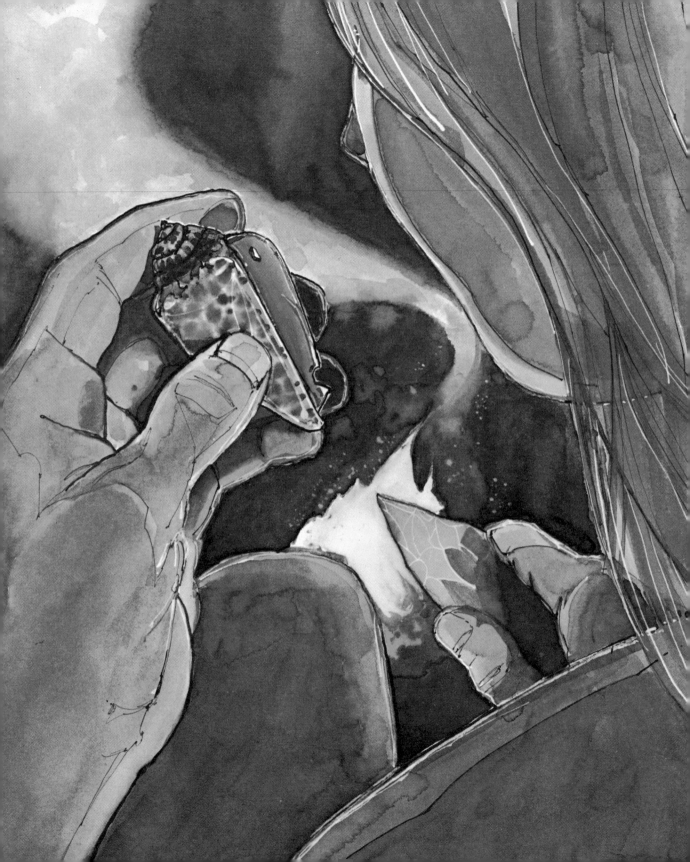

He took the string from around his neck and untied it carefully. He was adding the new shell to the collection when a shadow fell across the cave entrance. Targ looked up.

His mother stood watching him just inside the doorway.

"So you're at it again, Targ!"

Targ was embarrassed. He tied the string and slipped it hastily back around his neck.

"Our cave needs food," his mother scolded. "And what does Targ do? He plays with shells!"

"Yesterday I brought berries—" Targ began.

"Berries?" his mother scoffed. "We need meat! And there is so little to be found. Your brother Muga is called 'Keen Eye,' for he spots reindeer when there are reindeer to be found. Your brother Ti is called 'The Hare Catcher,' for he is quick to catch hares if there are hares to be found. But you, Targ—" She shook her head sadly. "They give you no hunter's name. They call you 'The Shell Hunter.' You bring only berries and look for shells!"

His mother came into the cave, but Targ did not look at her. He stared unhappily at the fire.

"Your brothers are with the other men making ready to hunt," she told him. "Now go and join them."

Targ nodded and left the cave in a hurry. The wind had grown very cold. Another covering of hides would have felt good around his body. But Targ had no wish to go back into the cave to get them.

The other men and boys had already gathered on the open meadow below the caves. They would soon march south. They hoped as always to find a stray elk or bison on the more open plains. Even if they were lucky, though, Targ knew they would return with only a few birds or perhaps some hares.

For many years game had grown more scarce. Each winter seemed longer and colder than the last. When snow came to the plains again—and that would be soon—there might be no food at all. Targ feared that his people must soon leave their homes and move southward if they were to stay alive.

Targ went down to join the others. When the hunting party moved forward, he tagged behind for a while.

They soon began to pass the tall, dark forest that rose to the left. Targ looked in that direction. The hunt seldom led there, for there were almost no animals left in the forest. It was thought that evil spirits had entered the forest and frightened the animals away. Some birds and smaller creatures remained in the upper terraces, but they always moved beyond the reach of stone or club.

There were still acorns, nuts, and a few clumps of berries among the giant trees, though. If Targ's brothers were not successful on today's hunt, these would be most welcome.

Targ lagged more behind. At last, when he was sure no one was looking, he ran to the forest.

Targ liked the forest. He knew its dangers and he knew his own people feared its darkness. But he had always liked it.

For a time he wandered among the giant pines and oaks. Now and then he came upon clear, trickling brooks. Their musical waters were as cold as ice. Each time he searched carefully for shells.

In the darkest nooks, large snowbanks clung to the moss-covered rocks. The snow in these places had been building higher each winter. The heat of the short summer sun was not strong enough to melt them completely. Some of the snowbanks were older than Targ could remember.

Under the snow's thin outer crusts Targ found a few nuts and acorns. These he put into a leather pouch that hung from his belt.

21

By mid-afternoon, Targ had climbed up into the center of the forest. There the forest was split by a deep, narrow gap. He walked south along the edge of the gulf, or chasm. He knew that soon he would come to the high cliffs where the two halves of the forest ended. The cliffs there fell away to the endless plains below.

Two trees, uprooted by a storm, lay across the deep chasm a few yards away from the cliff edges. These trees formed a bridge over the chasm. Targ had often wanted to crawl across the trees to the other half of forest. They looked rotten beneath their thick matting of moss, vines, and leaves, though. He was afraid to trust them.

For a while Targ gazed out over the yellow plains. He remembered stories the older clansmen had told at night around the cave fires. They spoke of days of their own youth. Then there had been great hunts—long ago when herds of bison, horses, and even camels had roamed these very plains. Now nothing stirred. Targ soon tired of watching.

25

For fun he lay flat on his stomach and moved out over the chasm. He squirmed farther and farther—just to see how far he could go without falling.

He soon spotted a ledge on the rock wall below. He stopped to study it. When his eyes were used to the darkness below, he gasped. A bush was growing on the ledge—a bush loaded with fat berries! In his excitement, Targ almost fell over the edge of the chasm.

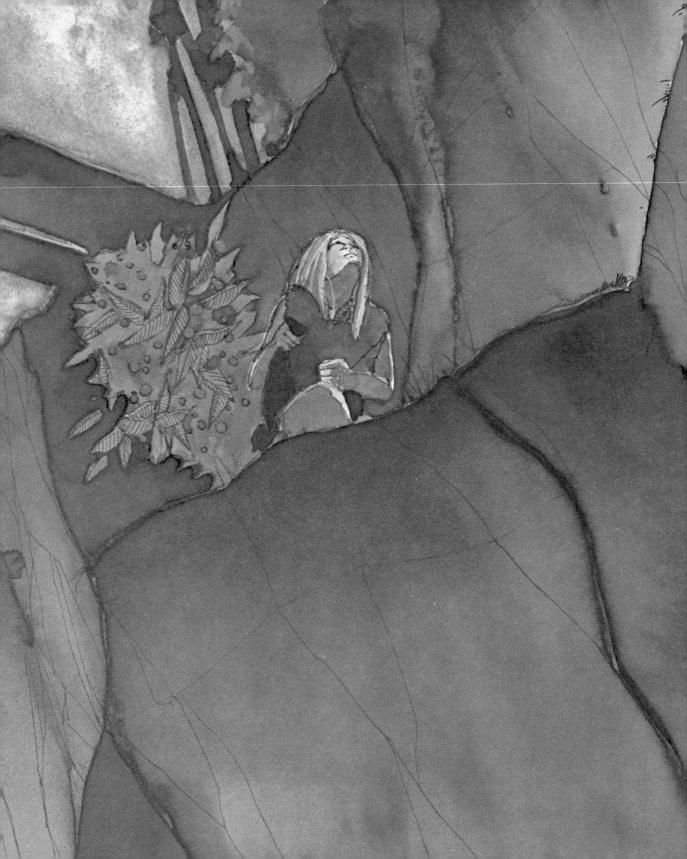

Targ lowered himself carefully onto the ledge and squatted beside the bush. He tasted the berries. They were delicious! The best and juiciest he had ever tasted! He ate his fill of them. Before filling the leather pouch to carry home, he leaned back and studied the chasm from this strange, new angle.

It was very still in the shadows. No trickle of brooks, no rustle of leaves could reach his ears. He peered over the ledge and saw a ribbon of white ice far below him at the bottom of the gulf. That was a river in warmer times, he thought.

A sudden snapping of twigs frightened him. He looked up in alarm. Something was nearing the edge of the chasm—something *big!*

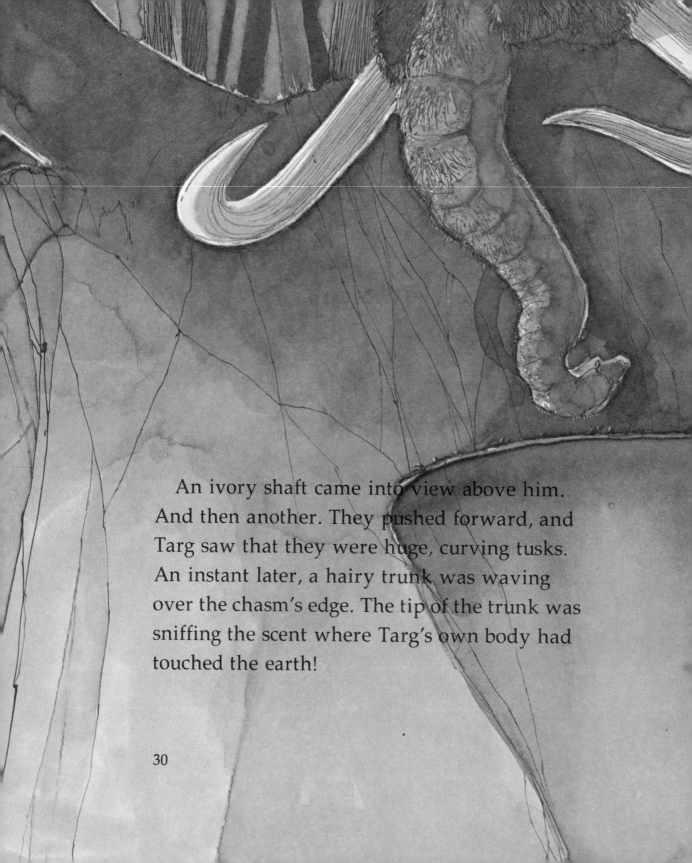

An ivory shaft came into view above him.
And then another. They pushed forward, and
Targ saw that they were huge, curving tusks.
An instant later, a hairy trunk was waving
over the chasm's edge. The tip of the trunk was
sniffing the scent where Targ's own body had
touched the earth!

30

Targ caught his breath in terror. A wooly mammoth! It had been years since he had seen one of these huge beasts. Even then, he had not been nearly as close!

Where had it come from? When had it come into this abandoned forest? It had followed Targ's trail, he was sure! How else could it have known he was inside the chasm?

The trunk paused briefly. Then it came slowly down the wall toward his head. Targ looked beyond the ledge. There was no way down, no footholds along the rocks. The drop was far too long. He was a prisoner on the tiny shelf of rock.

The trunk dipped lower. Targ stretched out flat on his back. That was all he could do. He saw the trunk drifting over his head. He realized that it could come no farther. But if the animal should kneel—

Instead, the trunk went back up the wall, then disappeared. But the terrible tusks remained. They started a gentle swaying motion over the chasm. The mammoth was waiting!

It seemed like hours that Targ lay flat on the ledge watching the swaying tusks. The sunlight dimmed. The shadows in the chasm became blacker. The cold made Targ numb.

As time passed, he began to think more clearly. The first moments of terror were gone. He began to realize what the discovery of the wooly mammoth could mean. If the beast could be killed, there would be more food than his clansmen had seen in a very long time.

He shifted his head so he could see the open end of the chasm. He could see the plains beyond it. Targ knew that his brothers and the rest of the hunting party would soon return that way. He hoped they would pass near enough to hear him yell.

The sun went down and moonlight flooded the plain. Finally, the hunt party came into view. At first they looked to Targ like faraway shadows. When he realized they were people, he gave a mighty yell. It echoed in the darkness, but they did not hear.

He tried again.

After the third try, he had an idea. Muga had once scolded him for the shrill, piercing noise of his larger shells. Wouldn't this noise carry farther than his own voice? If Muga and Ti heard such a noise from the forest they would guess what it meant—brother Targ in trouble!

Targ placed three of the largest shells to his lips and blew very hard.

The shadows paused!

He blew again—a longer blast. Then he whistled out a pattern.

He saw the shadows start running, and breathed a sigh of relief.

Waiting was easier now. From time to time he blew again on the shells. That was to guide the hunt party in the right direction.

He heard their faint cries even before he saw the torchlight on the leaves high overhead.

It was a mighty battle, but Targ only heard it. Clubs and stones whistled past him in the darkness. Amid the cries and shouts there was wild trumpeting, snorting, and pawing of earth. Targ knew the hunters had cornered the beast directly above him. In the darkness, though, he could not tell how the battle was going.

Then suddenly there was a great shaking noise. Earth, rocks, and leaves fell past Targ. He hugged the wall. Something large hurtled past him with a *whoosh!* Seconds later he heard the heavy thud as the mammoth struck the chasm floor.

Warm torchlight spread over the ledge. Targ heard voices.

"Targ? Targ? Where are you, little brother?"

There were fires in the great central cave that night. There was feasting and chanting and laughter—the first Targ remembered in a long, long while.

But tonight there was no talk of olden days. Instead, the clansmen talked only of the recent battle. They told over and over how Targ had led them to such a glorious prize.

Wonderful were those words spoken by the chief clansman.

"Tonight," he said, "little Targ has brought us the food we have needed so badly. He has also shown us wisdom in the ways of the hunt. In the past we hunted in packs, like the wolf. But by taking these tiny shells we may now scatter to the winds. Thus, we will increase our chances of finding game. The voices of the shells will let us know when game is found and if help is needed. If Targ will make such voices for each of us, we will be proud to own them. 'The Shell Hunter' is a wise and mighty one."

Even Targ's mother smiled at the name—for there was great respect in the chief's voice when he said it.

About the Author:

Carl Geren was born and raised in the beautiful Ozark coun-
try of southwest Missouri. Following high school, and some
time spent in the Air Force with a bit of roving around, he en-
rolled at Southwest Missouri State University in Springfield,
Missouri. Movies and movie making have always been a
source of fascination for Mr. Geren, so upon completion of col-
lege, he naturally migrated west—to the magic land of Hollywood. During his years in Hollywood he worked as a freelance commercial artist and magazine writer, with occasional
digressions into studio script work and acting as an extra in
movies. A few years ago, Mr. Geren returned to the Ozarks to
continue his work as a commercial artist and writer. He began
writing children's stories for national magazines in 1962, and
found it a most rewarding experience. *Shell Hunter* is his first
book for children, but he has plans for many many more.

About the Artist:

John Maggard was born in North Carolina and grew up in
Ohio. He received his Bachelor of Fine Arts degree from
Miami University in Oxford, Ohio. He now works as a
freelance illustrator, and has won awards for his work. Mr.
Maggard's major interest, other than art, is music. He plays the
piano, guitar, and banjo.

a